T0196447

PLEASED
TO MEET YOU...

PLEASED TO MEET YOU...

ROBERT ROSELLI

PLEASED TO MEET YOU...

iUniverse books may be ordered through booksellers or by contacting:

iUniverse
1663 Liberty Drive
Bloomington, IN 47403
www.iuniverse.com
1-800-Authors (1-800-288-4677)

Because of the dynamic nature of the Internet, any web addresses or links contained in this book may have changed since publication and may no longer be valid. The views expressed in this work are solely those of the author and do not necessarily reflect the views of the publisher, and the publisher hereby disclaims any responsibility for them.

Any people depicted in stock imagery provided by Thinkstock are models, and such images are being used for illustrative purposes only. Certain stock imagery © Thinkstock.

ISBN: 978-1-4917-9585-9 (sc)
ISBN: 978-1-4917-9586-6 (e)

Library of Congress Control Number: 2016907182

Print information available on the last page.

iUniverse rev. date: 05/03/2016

This book is dedicated to two groups. The first is comprised of those who have given their lives in the protection of this once Godly nation against all enemies without. This encompasses General and President George Washington, the greatest American that ever lived, to the faceless private who never made it home from Iwo Jima. On the flip side, it is dedicated to "Them" and their predecessors. Today "They" are the Rockefeller-Kissinger-Brzezinski-Soros led UN-American Genocidal Complex and their enigmatic sun of god "President" Barrack Obama who have taken it from within thereby negating the Divine and selfless efforts of the first group. Congratulations to you worshippers of Baal, modern day money-changers, Communist sellouts and "cosmic messengers" on the accomplishment of your "Great" Plan for your "Great" Society. You've won.

And the best of luck with Mother Russia, Red China and the religion of peace not to mention your upcoming trial before the Supreme Judge of the world; you're going to need it.

INTRODUCTION

———— ❁ ————

This is a "fictional" conversation in which Orwell's *1984* merges with John Carpenter's *They Live* and *In the Mouth of Madness* while Mick Jagger's "Sympathy for the Devil" plays in the background. In *1984*, Winston, the main character, is interrogated by a Party member named O'Brien after the former is caught in an illicit love affair, hence the name of my fictional character. Mr. Orwell's book is genuinely depressing, primarily for two reasons. One, as will be discussed carefully throughout the story, it describes to a T the situation we find ourselves on the brink of here in this once-great nation – and in fact the world – as is also predicted in the Book of Revelation. Two, Orwell doesn't believe in the saving grace of God through his Son Jesus Christ. This means there's *no* hope for mankind whatsoever except a descent into the endless abyss of a communistic system of government controlled by the compassionate Big Brother with its citizens even coming to love their slavery. There is no other logical conclusion one can arrive at absent the God of the Bible. It's all documented on my web site, www.boxofsunglasses.com, which I hope readers will consult, along with my other books, as the terms and names that arise in the "conversation" that is to follow have an all-too-literal relevance to my other works and can help provide a firm foundation from which to understand them-as well as the current events that continue to unfold towards an unspeakable climax of Biblical proportions.

The conversation is a figment of my imagination but the historical events that Mr. Obrien - who represents the real Establishment throughout history and our very own shadow government today in 2016 - and his associate, Mr. Khul, discuss are, unfortunately, as factual as they are disconcerting. This book was originally written in 2007, but little has changed in the past decade. Even the insults are direct quotations from those who've served as the forerunners and inspirations for many of today's pre-selected phony Progressive Presidential candidates and other liberal sell-outs who reside in "both" political parties that THEY have provided us.

Now let's take a look into the "Great" Plan of our very own criminal Illuminati elite as THEY attempt to usher in their very own "Great" Society. From here on in, discernment (read: Independent Thought) is key.

And remember, since you won't hear about this on The O'Reilly Factor and FOX News nor will THEY talk about it, this account is a totally fictional story by a lonely and kooky conspiracy theorist.

With that let's join Mr. Obrien and his friend who goes by the name Mr. Khul in their usual daily routine of numbing the masses to sleep in the fictional land of New Atlantis.

Except today a problem arises…

(TH)EverYthing is a LI(V)E

———— ❧ ————

I t's sometime in the future, around the early twenty-first century and the Party has been in control for some time. The wars never seem to end and the debt clock in Grimes Square is literally about to run out of digits as the New Atlantean government keeps trying to stimulate the economy. Mr. O'Brien is in charge of the Ministry of Information which is responsible for keeping the sleeping public in line. He transmits his message under the ever-watchful almost Illuminated eyes of his friend, Mr. Khul. This quiet yet charismatic man *seems* like he has the Party interests at heart and he always seems to be in the right place at the right time with the right answers.

So it is no surprise that there's a lot of confusion about the nature of Mr. Khul's game. Nobody knows where he came from and what his motives really are. And his age is an even bigger mystery. There is a not a soul anywhere, even amongst the Party elders, that can recollect a young Mr. Khul. Yet his physical appearance of an elderly well groomed gentleman of great wealth and taste hasn't changed one iota in several decades. The stories surrounding this man, some of which date back literally several centuries and some longer, can be neither confirmed nor denied. A person very similar to him appears in various history books while according to other references he exists only as a legend. Yet nobody dares to ask him if he is in fact this mystery person. Some claim he's from the region of Tibet or India while others say Egypt or Greece. Some in the Party have even speculated he is not even of this earth. And his always calm demeanor with a hint of smugness around the very powerful Party bosses indicates that he relishes his high position in the Party's power structure. In the midst of all the rumors and innuendo that swirl around the enigmatic yet somewhat elegant gentleman two things are well known yet rarely discussed and then only behind closed doors. One is that at some point anyone that wants to advance in the Party must bow and kiss the ring that resides on the finger of Mr. Khul. More importantly, the fate of anyone, even the most ardent Party loyalist, who comes under Mr. Khul's ire, is as mysterious as the man himself.

The Party and the compromised political system of lackeys, media moguls, academic experts and so-called evangelicals it rules over is the ubiquitous THEY the proles, or the bovine masses, constantly refer to as the ones who won't allow anything *really* bad to happen. But bad things continue to happen. The economy is riddled by debt and the burden of tens of millions of pathetic welfare cases even though the Ministry of Plenty was created to make everyone wealthy. The wars are perpetual even though the Ministry of Peace was created to end all wars. Most of the proles cannot even add or recall basic history even though the Ministry of Education was created to make everyone smarter. And the animosity amongst the proles themselves is ever present as they vie for control of trinkets, toys and other trivialities years after the Ministry of Love was initiated to distribute everything fairly and equally.

After years of Party loyalty Mr. O'Brien finds himself atop the Ministry of Information. In contrast to all the other Ministries which generally work in more methodical five year plans, the Ministry of Information has a more immediate function. It keeps the proles in line on a daily basis. If the masses ever had a chance to clear their minds and realize that they are little more than chained prisoners in a dark cave the Party's tenuous grip on power would evaporate overnight. The Ministry works to keep the proles mentally frozen in place with information overload via repetition of irrelevant news and endless entertainment. Hence it is arguably the most important Ministry of all. This relevance has not been lost on Mr. Khul. In fact, none of the Ministry of Information's truth – at least truth as the Party sees it - can be transmitted without Mr. Khul's approval. All information goes out subliminally via the Meru Antenna on top of the Ministry building located at 1 Crockefella Center in the middle of Metropolis. The subliminal messages are taken in by receptors at the education centers, major media conglomerates and news stations that are little more than lackeys for the Party, the real establishment. The Ministry of Information controlled media and universities comply by relaying the messages via live feed and print as they subliminally resonate from everywhere and anywhere including television sets, I phones, radios and beneath the print in the myriad of garbage news magazines, phony newspapers, overpriced textbooks and endless celebrity laden gossip rags.

As this constant sewer like spew of mind numbing commercials telling the proles to buy everything from toilet paper to expensive cars, entertainment gossip that is passed off as news and stupid television shows that are as pointless as they are endless THEIR mind control deception works beautifully. In fact things have gotten so bad the major Presidential candidates are pre-selected from the same pool of pro Big Brother buffoons as the "two" major political parties have essentially become merged. On the surface these pre-selected candidates seem to disagree. But because they say nothing in public except proposing change and what an idiot the other candidate is, the proles, with their now neutralized minds, really think their voice matters because they still have the right to vote for one of these morons. And any Presidential candidate or any elected official for that matter that dare speaks out or tries to enforce the dead Constitution that hasn't been put in the same cold state as the now meaningless document is mocked, laughed at and otherwise ignored by both the conservative and liberal experts. The experts are all postmodernist and disregard and mock the Founding Fathers; the same men who warned of what would happen to a Godless New Atlantis.

THEY, unlike the proles who sit at home and watch Atlantean Idle Minded every night after slaving away for THEM all day, are *never* idle as THEY have even selected the experts themselves to be the final say on the fake Presidential candidates. In summary, the Presidential election process for the supposedly most powerful person in the world has become a selection process by THEM and a literal joke as puppet string controlled useful idiots vie for control of nothing. This is all to the literal amusement of O'Brien and the Party who regard the tax-paying masses as the "imbecile majority" and "petty bourgeoisie".

Concurrently with the Presidential election scam the New Atlantis Parliament argues that someone might have smoked some joints while working at the very popular Metropolis Circus and then lied about it. This gets the proles talking about *something* but thanks again to the Ministry of Information's mind altering efforts few can remember that this is the same group of hypocrites, useless officials and morons that robbed its own bank and post office blind just a few short years ago. Also, Adam Spangreen, the public face for the mysterious Ministry of Plenty, is paraded out sporadically in front of the proles with nuggets of wisdom on the economy. Everyone, even the proles, realize that he and his henchmen really run the economy but they still don't get what a contradiction this is in a supposedly free country. This is because they are under mass mind control and have been convinced to believe that this must be since THEY are doing it in their interest to never allow anything really bad to happen like say another "Great" Depression. Outside of a few conspiracy kooks nobody in the sheep like mass bothers to ask how it is acceptable that THEY own the falsely labeled Government Bank. Therefore, it is THEY who have the real power to make or break the economy and therefore the nation. In reality this means that THEY have already staged a coup in the formerly great United Sta.. umm New Atlantis and control events to THEIR benefit. The Constitution now holds as much weight as an old Superman comic and its Christian authors are given even less respect. Yet, after years of subliminal messages and media spewed nonsense, none of this resonates with the enslaved bovine proletariat.

In summary, this whole situation is funny to O'Brien and the Party, as the huddled masses have become historically ignorant, mind numbed herded masses that actually think they have a choice in where they get their information, political choices and entertainment. Soon the New Atlantis will be gone having immersed itself into a financial and moral morass not unlike the Roman Empire. And a new Oceania will rise from the ashes to be part of the Party's "Great" Plan.

Or so Mr. O'Brien thinks.

HIS STORY

---◈---

The Ministry of Information's home in Crockefella Center is a large dull grey building that easily gets lost amongst the more impressive architecture surrounding it in downtown Metropolis. Row after row of monochromatic windows of tinted glass reach all the way to the 100th floor. In contrast to its chameleon like physical stature on the outside, the inside is an entirely different story. Nobody amongst the endless masses has any idea of the awesome amount of the Party's work that goes on behind those drab grey walls. And this is just how the Party likes it.

Room 101 is deep within the bowels of the Ministry of Information. Few Party members are authorized access to Room 101 and for good reason. It is the nerve center of the Party's mind control apparatus. Much of this apparatus was originally developed with the help of captured scientists from Eurasia, Oceania's last foe in the so-called war to end all wars. Powerful computers utilize highly complex algorithms to transcribe the Party's simple messages and embed them into small packets of data that get transmitted out through the Meru antennae on the roof.

Messages are sent out at different frequencies on different days. Receptors at all the major universities, news stations and media outlets are programmed to pick up the frequency that applies to their particular venue. Some messages are quite extensive like those meant for use by the professors or in the text books at the major universities. For example, it takes a lot of combined effort and careful manipulation by the Party to metaphorically lobotomize enough of the proles to convince them that they must go into debt to the Ministry of Plenty in order to get out of debt to the Ministry of Plenty. It seems almost blasé on the surface but everyone within the Party knows how much of its intellectual resources have gone in to dissuading the masses from utilizing simple logic and even simpler mathematics. And these efforts must be constantly cultivated and the manipulations continued ever so carefully amongst the university professors and their budding underlings, economic students who will be paid great sums of money to perpetuate the Ministry of Plenty's scam. As the proles continue to see the debt clock in Grimes Square spin skyward at mind numbing speed even more of these efforts will be needed to maintain the Ministry of Plenty's economic hold on the economy.

The Party also realizes it cannot have even the slightest hint of anyone questioning its rules and regulations. There can be no competition on the source human rights. The Party needs the power to grant the masses whatever rights they have. This means it also has the power to arbitrarily remove these rights as it sees fit. Therefore, the Ministry of Education has been tasked to expunge from the minds of the proles any form of religion and a Supreme Being who might have a set of laws that differ from those of the Party. This is accomplished in similar fashion to the Ministry of Plenty's debt scam. The Ministry of Education's Science Department conjures up endless studies that override outright impossibilities such as complete randomness creating perfect order and live beings arising from inanimate objects. The results of these studies are sent out by the Ministry of Information monthly and yearly and picked up by the media and universities. All of this results in textbooks, classrooms and magazines that are jam packed with Party supplied evidence that disproves the existence of a Supreme Being. No competing scientific viewpoints are allowed. Anyone that steps out of line and asks how it is the detailed anatomical drawings of an entire human can be extrapolated from a single tooth or how it is live beings can arise from the dead is derided and stripped of their employment to the point that they are forced out into the streets where a less than meager life and abject misery are the norm. Science has in essence accomplished the Party's goal to eliminate its main competition. But science and scientists don't grant and remove rights; this is the Party's job. And the Party does its job with a stone cold efficiency for the common good of the proles even if it means millions must be sacrificed for the elusive utopia that it seeks.

On the other hand, some of the Ministry of Information's messages are shorter and disseminated on a daily basis. The shorter messages mostly go out to the media outlets and news stations. Some of these messages include daily debate on the need for the endless wars that have no stated goal, nuggets of the Ministry of Plenty's wisdom on the economy, and coverage of useless entertainment. Sometimes the packets of information are adjusted ever so slightly by the various news stations to keep the proles from discerning that all their news comes from the same source. And some messages are simply repeated verbatim by the well groomed mimbos and painted on dress wearing bimbos in front of the cameras. Other messages are displayed as the mimbos and bimbos babble on about irrelevant stories that are packaged as legitimate news. This latter type is either passed along the bottom of the screen or embedded in the endless silliness and abject stupidity that passes off as advertising. Get the latest car, fly the fanciest jets, take the finest vacations, watch your sporting events or invest with us and don't worry about the economy it's all an "endless cycle".

The major media outlets include nationwide television station NTC, "Nothing To C here" and entertainment giant ViaCommunism "We entertain reality right out of you with our reality". Meanwhile 24 hour news channels conservative The FIX is in NEWS whose slogan is "We distort, you take the ride", and the liberal CommunistNewsNetwork, the "Most busted name in news" are the two main news choices. Right now THEY provide the mind numbed enslaved masses or proles with manufactured news stories that keep their minds off what's really happening and endless coverage of pre-selected choices of who THEY want for President. False information from the Ministry of Plenty is fed to the Ministry of Information that in turn makes sure it is transmitted around the clock on CircusNTC, where "Our clowns are the best clowns". The Circus spews an endless stream of fake government statistics and other nonsense while they squabble about everything but actually say nothing. The print media gets in on the act as well as all the papers take their cue from the Metropolis Slimes, "Where we honor our evolutionary forefathers".

But it cannot be emphasized enough that it is of the utmost importance that the proles don't catch on to the fact that the supposedly free and independent press is all held in the common ownership of the Party.

Today's particular group of messages is aimed at the news stations. The Party is becoming very concerned that its biggest scam, the Ministry of Plenty, is about to be exposed by some rabble rousers that occasionally crop up amongst the proles. These conspiracy theorists must be dealt with post haste.

Right now join O'Brien as he deceives the masses once again with his daily broadcast from Room 101.

After reviewing the day's Party approved messages and commercials O'Brien leaves his office atop Crockefella Center. Mr. Khul, who is always prompt, meets up with him in the empty hallway. After a brief exchange the two get onto the elevator. They take the trip all the way down to Room 101 without another word passing between them.

After exiting they walk briskly to their destination. The two flash their passes in front of the biometric reader and the first door opens. A guard sits at a desk as both men are fingerprinted before being allowed entry into Room 101. Mr. O'Brien takes his usual seat and uploads the Party's information. The daily newscast gets transmitted first.

"The wars and surveillance both here and abroad have to continue. We simply have to make the world safe for democracy. People need to experience the good life we have here in New Atlantis. We are the exceptional people and the uneducated people throughout the world must be brought up to speed. This means that as difficult as it on all of Oceania the war spending must continue. People must continue to pay their taxes. Or they're simply not being patriotic. And of course the Ministry of Plenty will always be there with sufficient monies to supplement all our taxes because of course we simply must continue all the other obligations of the Party. Some of our sons and now our daughters might not come home alive or with all their faculties but this is the price of spreading a unique freedom and democracy like ours while living in a dangerous world. Collateral damage is another sacrifice by all these people in these foreign lands. They don't know how miserable their lives really are so unfortunately many are expendable. This is another negative side but in spreading our innate goodness it is a price they must pay. And these enemy countries simply must stop harboring all those terrorists. We must eliminate this terroristic threat even if it means suspending all our basic rights at home for as long as it takes. The DHStasi is doing a fine job of eliminating all terrorists be it those who hate us because of the all the freedoms we now enjoy even if many of those freedoms are now restricted as a result of the war or, just as important, those citizens of New Atlantis who dare question any of the Party's Ministries here at home. The worst of these offenders might be those that question whether the Ministry of Plenty has any money at all and, get this; some of these domestic extremists even question whether there is any gold at all in the Party's main depository at Fort Krox (LAUGHTER). In all seriousness, we simply cannot have dangerous extremists out there questioning the noble motives of the Party. The way I see it these domestic extremists, by undermining the Ministry of

Plenty's sincerity and credibility, are every bit as dangerous to our way of life as those that hate us because of our freedoms. And they must be dealt with in similar fashion."

"The wars and surveillance both here and abroad have to continue."

"According to the latest numbers from the Ministry of Plenty the unemployment rate officially hit 0.0% last week. This was explained by Hurverd College economics expert Laurence Winters, who opined on the good news. "Those that are working continue to work so they can be counted in both the numerator and denominator of the employment equation. Those that are not working are now extricated from the denominator because they are out of the workforce and can therefore be discarded. Hence we can now divide the number of workers working by the total membership of the workforce. This gives us the great news, 100% employment. This of course is the mathematical way of saying 0.0% unemployment which sounds better politically. And we all know how politicians love to massage these things to their benefit during an election season (LAUGHTER). All kidding aside we can now see the president's policies along with constant assistance in the form of monetary relief and expert advice from the Ministry of Plenty are having a really positive effect on the overall economic picture. And this bodes well for all the college grads coming out who will have to pay for their very expensive educations."

"And there was more campaigning today. Joe Bloe inquired how Fredding Mooron can be Minister never having served in any Ministry. "How can he implement important bills for the people?" Mr. Bloe put out on the blogosphere. Mr. Mooron replied," Joe Bloe wears pink underwear and I have the photos to prove it." None of the candidates had anything to say about the endless wars, violent crime exploding amongst the impatient population, skyrocketing public and private graft, drug addictions, university seniors that can't add, rampant diseases coming in from foreign lands or the ongoing nuclear meltdown in Eurasia. And neither of the leading candidate had anything to say about the good economic news as they have no interest in complimenting the current regime."

"In entertainment news Viacommunism came out with another Moon Wars movie. In a few moments we'll bring in many of the actors and actresses on this thirteenth part in what was originally forecast as a trilogy when the first one came out almost 40 years ago. As you can see this shot only two blocks from our studios the throngs have been lining up for days to get tickets for the premiere. The actors will get into important issues like what it's like to shoot a fake ray gun at fake actors in a fantasy movie that has no bearing on our lives except for around five and a half hours it allows us to escape the everyday stresses of life like working enough to keep the IRSS and the Ministry of Plenty from seizing a bank account or changing the locks on your doors."

O'Brien then uploaded the commercials with their subliminal messages.

If you're hungry Sub(MIT)Shop has a (WATCH) T(V)wo for On(B)e(Y) deal. Thank you f(CONF)or(M) co(NSU)ming.

Don't forget to pay your taxes(TAY ASLEEP). O(BEY)r the (NO) I(NDEPENDENT THOUGHT)RSS will come get you. But we at Chuck S(TAY)lobs can (AS)h(L)e(E)p you with yo(BEY)ur IRSS problems. Just pay us and w(ATCH) e'll make sure t(V)he Ministry of Plenty's goon squads leave you alo(B)ne(Y) for at least six months guaranteed(ON'T QUESTION AUTHORITY).

Don't Q(U)estio(N) the Exper(AUTHORI)t(Y)s on the econo(BEY)my. It's (WATCH) t(V)oo co(NFOR)mplex for you. Stop by o(BEY)our offices at Bank of Atlantis for investment help. Yo(U)'re (N)ot educated enough to save for yourselves. S(UBMIT)ave y(OUR) money to us. It will be in go(BEY)od hands .

(SU)b(MIT)uy some more to (ST)imul(AY ASLEEP) te the econ(OBEY)my. Shop at Sky-Mart fo(BEY)r all the l(W)at(CH)est(V) savings.

Be smart and be Pro(BEY)gressive with a Vote for Hill(STA)r(Y) (ASLEEP). "I say be su(BMIT)re to igno(B) re(Y) those kook cons(UME)piracy theorists, those rac(ONSFORM)ist Min(U)teme(N) and those Christian extrem(ARRY AND REPRODUCE)ists. They are just(AY ASLEEP) a bunch of freaks(UBMIT)". (WE ARE THEY AND WE RULE).

Then it happened.

O'Brien went into a sudden fit of rage and could not help himself. He broke off in the middle of the commercial upload with a spontaneous outburst as he ranted, "Christians, what a bunch of morons."

The usually quiet and unassuming Mr. Khul, who never showed emotion of any sort, uttered an immediate warning in a slightly elevated tone.

"Excuse me Mr. O'Brien you're leaving the script and the Party is listening."

But O'Brien's anger took on a momentum that overrode both his own inhibitions as well as the protests of Mr. Khul.

O'Brien continued, "Who do they think they are? Jesus Christ as ruler of all humanity. **We** rule Humanity. Not him. **Us**. I hate them with all my heart. I hate them. I hate them. I hate them."

Mr. Khul, who was struggling to maintain the steady composure that he was known for said, "I know sir, I hate them more than you believe me, but you must stick to the script and you must maintain control of yourself."

But Mr. O'Brien rambled on. "We are **They**. **We** Control the Press. **We** let them know whom they're allowed to vote for. **We** own the banks. **We're** god. Didn't **We** get rid of these dogmatic weeds with the theory of evolution? An egg started the universe. Duh. Most of these profane savages will buy anything, except those nauseating Christians."

The usually well composed Mr. Khul was now becoming visibly annoyed as he tried to assert himself. "Umm… Mr. O'Brien you should really shut up now."

Even under the now forceful protestations of Mr. Khul the unrepentant O'Brien would not stop as he continued to opine, "We need more effort from the Ministry of Truth. And what happened to the Ministry of Education? They simply must do better. We need to convince that what we say is gospe…well you know what I mean. It worked perfectly with those lunatic environmentalists. Now we've got the whole world ready to bow to us to save it from itself just like the bunch of mundane imbeciles they really are."

"Sir..please," replied Mr. Khul in his most elevated voice yet.

But O'Brien went on as he blurted about Big Brother's environmental scams which were thinly veiled efforts at top-down control of every facet of the proles' sorry existence.

"Global warming? Is the petty bourgeoisie really that gullible? It just snowed in Baghdad for Go...goodness sakes. Thirty years ago we had the whole population believing we were about to freeze to death! Fine; just switch the name to climate change and these savage proles will *still* be with this. Well that shouldn't surprise me....fifteen years ago we got the whole world to ban those CFCs...they're heavier than the air for Chri...sake. Haven't these yokels even heard of gravity? They *all* buy into this garbage almost too easily... except those putrid Jesus freaks..."

Mr. Khul, realizing he was letting his own emotions get the better of him, searched for the right words but could only get out "Mr. O'brien. Sir..." before O'Brien continued his unscripted and highly illegal rant.

If blurting out in an uncontrolled setting about the environmental scam was bad then what O'Briend had to say next was a hundred times worse. "Jesus Christ returning to the earth to rule forever? Yeah if you buy that one I've got a private bank that really runs New Atlantis *and* world economies to sell you."

Mr. Khul was losing control of the situation so he quickly replied, "Mr. O'Brien you should really shut up now, we set that up already. If the proles actually woke up and figured out the whole economy is really a set up and the Ministry of Plenty is bankrupt we're screwed. (Reminder to self, when I'm done with O'Brien here I have to go have a word with this new Chairman Burrnaki shooting his mouth off how the Ministry of Plenty really did cause the Great Depression)."

Mr. Khul continued as he snarled, "You of all people should know it is unauthorized and highly illegal to speak

ANY state secrets outside of Party Headquarters. Now I admonish you to cease and desist and get back to uploading the daily messages."

O'Brien agreed for a brief moment. In a tone still reflective of his sour mood he managed a half-hearted "okay, okay."

Not surprisingly O'Brien ramped up the verbiage once again. "**We** own them and they actually think they're free. What audacity. And get rid of these Christians. Everyone is in line, our line, except for them. If the proles and the rest of the imbecile majority need some kind of religion in their free time we let them have when they're not working to pay our usury interest charges then let them go worship the umpteenth dalai lama with those New Age Eastern Religions or kill each other to get to heaven like those Muslims with that bloodthirsty beheading prophet what's his name?…Mohammed. Or better yet let 'em go worship Mother Earth with those jerk-offs over at the Ministry of Peace."

Mr. Khul could barely get out his next request as he uttered to no avail, "Mr. O'Brien, please refrain from saying too mu…."

But O'Brien continued spewing more state secrets. "Get those Christians off my back. And get rid of those documents you know the ones about rights coming from god and all that. **We** grant them their rights. **We** can't rule with that god stuff still out there. They're trying to expose us like that repugnant Senator McCarthy almo…."

Mr. Khul, who remembered how close the Party's mechanisms of control came to being exposed jumped in without allowing O'Brien to finish. "Mr. O'Brien, sir, please don't bring his name back up...you remember how hard it was to squash that irritant," he told the now loose lipped O'Brien.

Yet O'Brien continued. "If you can't get rid of them legally than get the Ministry of Education or National Education Association or whatever it's called now to flush them down the memory hole."

Mr. Khul, whose usually calm demeanor was beginning to buckle, demanded, "Sir, please cease and desist...."

But O'Brien kept going. "Let everyone believe this Jesus split to France with his whore girlfriend Mary. Or he was just some regular guy. Let 'em think the founders were a bunch of backward white males who were infinitely evil. Or skip teaching them all together; whatever it takes."

Mr. Khul was now forced to issue a stern warning. "Mr. O'Brien...I wouldn't keep talking if I were you...."

O'Briend cut him off mid-sentence as he blabbered on. "And then get the Atlantis Criminal Liberty Union to sue the rest of 'em of all back to the stone age...Make something up, I don't know *anything* to **Separate** them from their Christian roots. I don't care."

Mr. Khul managed to squeeze in the second half of his warning as he concluded, "....because the consequences will be severe to say the least."

But O'Brien simply went on. "Get rid of their free speech and call it something good that the rest of the imbeciles will buy. But make it look like **We** really care about someone else while making them look really bad. Sir...Please...Use the homosexuals and let's see... call it the Fairness Doctrine and prosecute them under something called Hate Crimes. The proles won't even know about it, the key is to keep it out of

Our newspapers. And when we can't keep it quiet anymore get **Our** editors to support it. The proles will argue about it a little, the few politicians who really speak up we can just lambaste as "insensitive" and in the end they'll listen to our "experts" and think everything is a okay just like they always do like good little sheep. Get the…."

Mr. Khul was done with the more subtle approach as he nakedly warned his babbling compatriot. "Mr. O'Brien, sir, you *really* need to shut the hell up *right* now and get back to the script or you WILL be dealt with most severely."

O'Brien, thinking his prominence within the Party guaranteed immunity against anything finally gave in with a few simple words. "Oh yes of course. Sorry Mr. Khul. Where was I?"

Watc(ONFORM)h (TV) "Atlantean Gladiators (UBMIT)" tonight at 8 O(BEY)clock

And tomorrow at 8 O(BEY)clock don't miss the Myst(A)ery (ASLEEP) Channel where they'll discuss the quackery going around about that symbol on the back of those o(BEY)ne dollar bills you all s(UBMIT)pend everyday (LIKE THE IMBECILES YOU REALLY ARE) with that pyramid(ON'T QUESTION AUTHORITY) and that eye. That's n(O INDEPENDENT)t(HOUGHT) a direct sign fr(C)o(NSU)m(E) us with the phrase (NEW ORDER FOR THE AGES) about ho(BEY)w we (HAVE A GREAT) plan on ruling the w(ATCH TV)orld.

That was it for today. O'Brien logged off the computer system. He and Mr. Khul gathered their belongings and headed out the door and back to the elevator.

As the two walked past the guard's desk and down the dimly lit concrete hallway towards the elevator O'Brien, now completely oblivious to the possible ramifications of his uncontrolled rant a few minutes back, turned to Mr. Khul and in a jovial tone remarked, "I can't believe this garbage works. Just keep feeding them endless drivel out of those idiot boxes and "smart" phones and they become live zombies ready to fall for anything. We almost have the whole world under our grasp. These suckers will buy or do we mean by anything," as he laughed at his own little joke.

Mr. Khul, who was not at all amused, simply stared at O'Brien with a piercing look that belied his otherwise cool and collected demeanor.

The ring signaled the arrival of the elevator and the doors opened.

Then there was an uncomfortable silence as O'Brien's jocular and nonchalant mood ran head on into Mr. Khul's beady and serious eyes that seemed to stare right through O'Briens skull and onto the gray steel wall of the elevator behind.

O'Brien, who for the first time ever was at a loss for words, tried to break the quietness that while lasting only a few moments seemed like it went on for hours. So he blurted out something buried deep in his subconscious; something that really did not need to come out at this very moment. But it was as if Mr. Khul himself had willed it out of him. "You know I've been thinking about something Mr. Khul."

Mr. Khul, who instinctively knew what O'Brien was going to ask, replied simply, "What is it Mr. O'Brien?"

O'Brien came right out with it. "We spend all this time together; your opinions always seem to be right on, the Party *always* agrees with you and I'm *still* confused about the nature of your game. In fact everyone is puzzled by you."

"Fair enough," replied Mr. Khul. "Why don't we stop by my office for a moment?"

So the two stepped off the elevator and made their way to the corner office. The office was as plain and mysterious as its occupant. With the exception of a few paintings of famous revolutionary leaders of yester year the walls were painted a dull white and completely bare. On the opposite side of the room from the doorway, an old mahogany desk was located in front of a large window that looked down onto Grimes Square.

Then, fully anticipating what would happen next, Mr. Khul in a most subtle fashion glided over towards the mostly bare mahogany desk. It was at that precise moment that the only object on top of the desk, a small black phone with a direct line to Party Headquarters, rang out.

As Mr. Khul turned to answer he courteously pardoned himself. "I beg your pardon, Mr. O'Brien."

"Good morning, Mr. Khul here."

O'Brien feigned interest in the few murals of the great revolutionaries of yesteryear that hung on the office's drab walls. But he was trying to pick up snippets of the voice on other end of the phone; a voice that was very animated and more than a little annoyed.

But Mr. Khul said nothing in response that would allow O'Brien to ascertain the contents of the conversation.

"Yes," Mr. Khul replied. Then he listened for a moment and said, "I concur. Mmm hmm. I will deal with him, please calm down…Yes, I agree. Gentlemen please… have I ever let you down?"

Then Mr. Khul courteously concluded, "Good afternoon". He stared down at the desk for a brief moment of contemplation and he calmly put the phone back in its place.

The very curious O'Brien quickly quizzed, "Who was that? And needs to be dealt with now?" He hadn't a clue as to what was about to happen.

Mr. Khul came right out with it. "It was the Party, they are very unhappy with your recent rant. We were discussing *you*. That's top secret information and we simply cannot afford another emotional outburst like that. If the wrong person in one of our media outlets ever heard what you said and transmits your rant to the proles we're finished. *You* must now be, shall we say, "dealt with", Mr. O'Brien."

"Bull...There's nothing secret here," O'Brien immediately snapped back.

Mr. Khul calmly replied, "No, Mr. O'Brien, I disagree. And you said it yourself, the Party *always* agrees with me."

O'Brien beginning to sense that maybe he was not untouchable as he thought replied in a more conciliatory tone, "Come on Mr. Khul, the proles can go out and research most of the stuff themselves off one of those books we let them buy out of those book chains that dot the land like those fast food joints. And what we barely hide in all those books we shove right down their throats while they sit there and gaze around like a bunch of stunned deer in the headlights. They should be able to figure this out *sometime...* so it doesn't matter what I said."

Mr. Khul took a breath and explained, "That's exactly the point, Mr. O'Brien. You should know *my* whole Great Plan depends on the proles staying in their media induced drunken mental stupor that you and I so carefully ferment day after day."

After a brief pause Mr. Khul then walked to the window behind his desk and looked down. O'Brien, noticing the wry smile and face that implied a deep reminiscing, kept his silence.

For a few moments Mr. Khul stared down at the unwashed masses hustling around below like so many worker ants. Then without moving a muscle and in his usual monotone voice but now with just a touch of glee he remarked, "Look at them all out there, so obedient. So malleable just like those seven metals of Alchemy I convinced those Babylonian and Egyptian fools to worship. They all just dilly-dally and walk around so busily yet at the same time lifeless. It would bring a tear to my eye if I could cry. It's just like my least hated movie, Night of the Living Dead. If they ever put the whole thing together they would shake us all right off like that horse did those flies in Mr. Orwell's book. One more rant like that just may get out, Mr. O'Brien. And you know damn well in the topsy turvy world we develop and maintain so meticulously every single day together everything is backwards; everything depends on the proles remaining asleep. Now we can call ourselves a host of names like progressive and tolerant while the only thing we *are* progressing towards is simply yet *another* dictatorship of the Illuminated privileged class for the enslavement of what's left of what we allow to live. And the only ones that could see this coming are the true progressives, those that started the concept of Atlantis and those damned Christians; a real government for the people, by the people, Mr. O'Brien, when the people actually used to think for themselves. Now thanks to us, the few that speak out we can just lambaste as kooks, crackpots and conspiracy theorists. Yes, Mr. O'Brien I hate those Christians much more than you'll ever know. But you lost control and said way too much over the airwaves with your little diatribe. And that is very dangerous indeed to *my* Great Plan, Mr. O'Brien."

O'Brien was now getting worried and asked simply, "What are you getting at Mr. Khul?"

Mr. Khul with no emotion whatsoever replied, "Unfortunately you must now be "dealt with" Mr. O'Brien."

O'Brien became more desperate as beads of sweat began to appear on his forehead. "But wait I run this very Ministry of Information. I practically invented the Ministry of Love. The Ministry o f Plenty was my brainchild. I *am* the Party."

Mr. Khul's reply was again terse and unemotional. "No Mr. O'Brien. You *were* the Party."

In contrast O'Brien began raising his voice. "No. No. No. You don't understand. I promoted Marx and Darwin; started Stalin and Lenin and the others. I'm the Party."

Mr. Khul paused for a second turned back from the window and simply and unemotionally replied, "Yes Mr. O'Brien, you are the Party. And now you *were* the Party."

O'Brien was really getting concerned about the direction of the conversation and became almost confrontational. "Wait a second; who are you really? You hang around the Party, you advise all its members what to do with some kind of weird charisma you have, you're always calm, and you act like a perfect gentleman yet you have never had to identify yourself or where you're from. Everyone in the Party hates and distrusts everyone else. But you, everyone seems to like. And trust. Are you with the Thought Police or something?"

Mr. Khul simply answered, "No Mr. O'Brien."

O'Brien kept guessing. "Then you must be with the Ministry of Plenty."

Again Mr. Khul stared unemotionally at the now profusely sweating O'Brien and muttered, "No Mr. O'Brien."

O'Brien's voice was shrill and desperate as he demanded, "Well then just who the hell *are* you, Khul?"

Mr. Khul, who was starting to enjoy O'Brien's meltdown, took on a somewhat sarcastic tone. "Funny you should ask, Mr. O'Brien. And funny you should use the word "hell". What's really puzzling you Mr. O'Brien, is the nature of my game. And that's "Mister" Khul to you."

Mr. Khul looked briefly at the ground and took a deep breath.

He looked back up and went on.

"Well at this point I believe it's safe to tell the truth, you've outlived your usefulness to me. Please allow me to introduce myself, Mr. O'Brien, I'm a man of wealth and taste. Many at the top of your very own Party have asked in the past. When they did have it figured out, like you, they were dealt with accordingly. Take that Lenin, one of our favorites, Mr. Obrien as he tried to have a change of heart there at the end. But he had already spawned that almost lovely Stalin fellow. It was too late for him or those tens of millions of poor bastards you, your Party and I screwed over. For me, if I were capable of love, I would have loved every moment of it. All that death and all that misery would make my heart flutter, if I had one. The Party *he* helped create had gotten way out of control. You, should know, Mr. Obrien. You, your friends and I were behind *him* and that Stalin.

You all *thought* you were in control. Not quite, Mr. Obrien. In this topsy turvy world of enigmas wrapped in mysteries all twisted in lies that we created together, I, the father of lies, am at the core. I am whom you were serving your whole life, Mr. Obrien, the "Angel of Light", so called."

O'Brien was obstinate as he shot back, "Whoa, wait a second here. I don't serve anybody. I rule the world. I will rule with an iron fist once again."

Mr. Khul's voice didn't waver in the least as he plainly replied, "Will you really, Mr. O'Brien? You are nothing to me. You are not unlike every other despot I have empowered throughout history. And while you were busy deceiving the whole world all this time, I was deceiving *you and the whole Party*, Mr. O'Brien. What puzzles you, Mr. O'Brien, is the nature of *my* game. A game I happen to be the best at."

O'Brien could say nothing as his mind began racing furiously.

Mr. Khul paused for a few seconds and then broke the silence. "We have a deal, Mr. O'Brien," he said in his usual calm tone that bordered on smugness.

O'Brien was now showing disrespect that was more a product of desperation than anything else. "Bull****; I never signed or agreed to anything with you "Mister" Khul."

In his calm manner Mr. Khul immediately responded, "Oh I respectfully disagree, Mr. O'Brien. When you gave up everything in your blind lust for power and bowed before me the Lord gave you to me. He did warn in the Bible we both hate so much yet continue to study that some would be given over to reprobate minds or me. Just like Him, when I get a soul tossed my way I tend to hang on with all my might. We are then locked in a deal, and I do mean *locked*.

It's no fun for me to let you know beforehand. Nonetheless I allowed you to live the good life, endless riches, power, and prestige and now it must come to end. I will collect. I *always* collect. And when you deal with me there are strings attached, my strings, Mr. O'Brien. Deceit and deal making with strings attached. Control and manipulation and trust nobody. You self proclaimed gentlemen *thought* you were the best. That's really the nature of *my* game you fool, you never did figure out whom you were really serving this whole time. The Lord didn't call me the "father of lies" for His health."

"You do understand what I am trying to convey here, don't you, Mr. O'Brien?"

Mr. Khul's question was rhetorical so he continued without allowing O'Brien time to garner a response.

"You know you could never have taken over the world without eliminating the evil system, evil from our point of view that is, those Godly men in that place you called your New Atlantis. They really did have it figured out for a while, didn't they, Mr. O'Brien? How if mankind would worship and listen to God he could really be prosperous and happy and helpful to his fellow man. *They* truly were a beacon of light that illuminated the world. But it stood in the way of *your* Party's lust for power, that one world utopia for you and 500 million of your chosen ones that you thought was *your* Great Plan. Then you, your friends and I figured out how to take it over without firing a shot. All those brave, faceless patriots in those - thanks to our Ministry of Education or whatever fancy name we gave it the National Education Association I believe - now forgotten places fighting and dying…Bunker Hill, the Alamo, Gettysburg, Midway, Bastogne…. In real wars somehow they always came through even after defeat...the most insurmountable odds...no desire for glory.... But we got them without firing a shot. If I could be proud... *that* act of deceit would make even me "A Shining One", Mr. O'Brien."

After all of today's events not to mention all the mystery and questions surrounding him, Mr. Khul succinctly and plainly stated, "If you must know, I'm the dark lord, Mr. O'Brien; Satan himself."

O'Brien, trying to camouflage his increasing desperation, sarcastically snapped, "Yeah right "Mister" Khul."

Mr. Khul continued to maintain his characteristic low key composure and replied, "Mr. O'Brien for once I speak with the utmost veracity. You never questioned me in the past so why don't you believe me now?"

O'Brien, desperately trying to keep up with Mr. Khul's superior wit and intelligence, shot back, "Well for starters, and don't take this personally, you look a little too human to me."

Mr. Khul then became inquisitive. "So Mr. O'Brien I take it that in all the time you spent looking through the Bible for your own personal gain and elixir of life you have never read about much less understood my encounters with Cain or that fool Judas Iscariot?"

To that O'Brien simply said, "Sorry to disappoint you Mr. Khul."

Mr. Khul lifted his hand to his face and pressed his lips with his index finger as he contemplated a more measured response. After a brief silence he spoke.

"Apparently I'm not getting through to you Mr. O'Brien. All that Bible reading looking for the answers to immortality and that Holy Grail really hasn't helped you out at all has it? Think about it this way Mr. O'Brien. Deep down you know God exists; it's written on the heart of every human as my former employee that Saul so plainly wrote. If God exists, perfect Goodness, than perfect evil, the exact opposite, must exist also or else neither has any meaning. That perfect evil would be *me*, Mr. O'Brien. But you chose to ignore Him and trade out now for control of the world's kingdoms. I control the world's kingdoms; at least for now. And I can offer them to whomever I want whenever I choose to. And as every so-called leader throughout history has learned I can also take it all away. I even showed Jesus Christ Himself every worldly kingdom in a moment of time and then offered them all to Him. All He needed to do was bow to me but He would not. You and your Party spent all that time studying the Scriptures looking to unlock the secrets of the Universe but you obviously missed this part. You should not have bowed to me."

In a bit of outright mockery Mr. Khul added, "Tisk, tisk, Mr. O'Brien."

O'Brien was beginning to wilt under the endless barrage of Mr. Khul's emotionless diatribes and stern facial expressions with those beady eyes that seemed to be reading his mind.

All he could get out was, "that gaze, it's so mesmerizing..."

Mr. Khul without missing a beat then shifted gears and came up with a question with no apparent relevancy to the conversation. "Do you like rock music, Mr. O'Brien?"

O'Brien, taken aback by the randomness of the question, answered, "Well... yeah. Before I had it all eliminated for the proles' own good that is."

Mr. Khul inquired, "Do you remember a song out of the sixties named "Sympathy for the Devil"?"

O'Brien responded with a simple "Yes."

Once again Mr. Khul pressed his lip which told O'Brien he was getting ready for a lengthy diatribe.

"Well Mr. O'Brien while we were busy fostering the counterculture movement and all that strife and lest I forget my almost favorite, the elimination of the Bible and God from the schools and eventually *all* of society, Mr. Jagger's song came out. And wouldn't you know that one song spoke more Christian truth than Mr. Jagger himself knew. After I tried to make Him mine I was indeed there when Jesus Christ had his moment of doubt and pain. I made Pontius Pilate wash his hands to seal His fate. We killed the czar and his ministers while Anastasia screamed in vain, didn't we Mr. O'Brien? That was the communist revolution for the people we started, Mr. O'Brien. With your friend Lenin and the Party, that small group of elite bankers who thought the world was some kind of self-gratifying monopoly board. It killed tens of millions and impoverished millions more. But it made you and your friends even richer and more powerful, didn't it Mr. Obrien? Then you didn't get "your" New World Order with what did we call our Ministry of Peace, Mr. Obrien? The League of Nations, was it not? So you and your friends helped some Bohemian madman rise to power, a real rock star in *my* book. Then you plunged the world into *another* world war. As Mr. Jagger sang I did ride a tank in the general's rank, Mr. Obrien. I was there. All that death and misery was *my* Great Plan in action. And *you* didn't even know it. And we got our Ministry of Peace didn't we Mr. O'Brien? What did we call it this time, The United

Nations? I proposed it, you paid for it, supported it, we had our media to hype it, you used it to lie about God's earth coming to some kind of environmental apocalypse, you had it all figured out didn't you, Mr. Obrien? Hell, pun most certainly attended, I even had some of those "New" Age fools doing my writing for me. I knew the writing would spread out like some unstoppable plague, constantly permeating, ever multiplying and infecting the world eventually driving it into the very mouth of madness. Quite simply, this is *my* Great Plan."

Mr. Khul gave his now quiet listener an opportunity to chime in. "What do you think, Mr. O'Brien?"

But O'Brien could only listen at this point and said nothing.

So Mr. Khul went on.

"I shouted out who killed the Kennedys, Mr. O'Brien. It *was* you and me wasn't it? And you helped me pull that off, didn't you, Mr. O'Brien? You got the people to believe that it was some magic bullet, a lone gunman; that was almost great. And boy did we go and do some real damage to God's favorite country, the good ol' New Atlantis. We got them into that war in some faraway country that caused tons of human misery, which if I haven't mentioned I just almost love by the way, fighting the very communism that we started and continued to support. Then we started something called a Great Society that has done nothing but make more slaves for the Party, bankrupted the country… and most importantly made you very wealthy. This was *supposed* to be our Great Plan but I was deceiving you while we were both supposed to be deceiving the proles; how twisted, how ironic, how backwards, how me."

Mr. Khul then asked, "And how can I forget that Woodstock? Talk about a symbol of *my* "New" Age, *my* "Age of Aquarius". Every spirit worshipping, Mother Earth loving, druggie was out for that one. And my cohorts and I were almost happy to accommodate every last one of them. They were espousing freedom ...supposedly. But their seemingly endless freedom without *any* rules can only lead to chaos and from chaos right back to despotism. Just like we knew all along Mr. O'Brien unbridled freedom is indeed the fastest way to anarchy then right to abject slavery. But we knew that many of them would filter into society, into our Ministry of Education, Ministry of Information, Ministry of Peace spreading their "New" Age beliefs... God would be further beaten out of society...crazy liberal laws...beat down the establishment....fight the power... moral relativism...everything is okay as long as you're not hurting anyone else...flowers of life...peace...love...joy...and then...the "New" Age...aaah. We had these hippies and those bought and sold universities, yet another branch of our ubiquitous Ministry of Education, fighting the very God we both despise so much. Yes of course it was He Who endowed them with what used to be their inalienable rights that granted them their *real* freedom in the first place. Soon we will have our anarchy at which time we'll have to step in and then *all* their rights will come from the Party. And of course we both now know who rules the Party. That one was almost too easy."

After sounding a bit elated Mr. Khul regained his more serious tone and confessed, "I can no longer enjoy wealth. I had it all but gave it all up for even more, or so I thought. You'll understand in a very short time. Wow, Mr. Obrien we've sure been busy. I'm *almost* sorry to see you go. You asked that poor chap, what was his name, Winston, if he believed in God. You *know* that God is the *only* power that can stop you and the Party and of course me at this point, don't you, Mr. O'Brien?"

O'Brien became completely speechless and could only mutter a simple "Uhhh."

Mr. Khul kept the pressure on the now slinking and increasingly pathetic O'Brien.

He continued, "Come on speak man. You were so cocky. Now look at you. You were going to rule the world. And what of those Godless Communists you helped me start? Do you think they're having second thoughts about *your* new world order, Mr. O'Brien? Do you think those Chinese and Russians are going to keep rolling over and playing dead like they have in the past, Mr. O'Brien? Or those Muslims, do you think Allah and his religion of peace followers approve of *your* "Great" Plan, Mr. O'Brien? The only way sure way to get to heaven is to kill oneself with as many infidels as possible. I almost love that kind of peace. They all will fight you to the most miserable deaths if I have my way. And I will have my way. Huge wars and massive death and misery are some of the things I hate least Mr. O'Brien. This is all part of *my* Great Plan."

Mr. Khul demanded, "Speak man; the floor is yours."

But O'Brien was still reeling as he was coming to the realization that everything that Mr. Khul was telling him was true. And he was sure this did NOT bode well for his future well being. Again he could only mutter, "Uhhh…"

Mr. Khul started once again.

"What is truth, Mr. O'Brien? You tried to eliminate it all together didn't you? You remember 2+2=5 and even better, you must go into debt to get out debt. I have to hand it to you Mr. O'Brien inventing the Ministry of Plenty and selling it, no pun intended, as the Federal Reserve Bank was some sleight of hand. You and Warburg and the boys got on that train and laughed it up about how you were going on some hunting trip. You invented that bank that has duped an entire great nation, great for those human vermin at least. All started under the watchful eye of the Almighty Himself way back there in 1776. And now you will tumble the world into economic chaos, chaos that you *thought* you could control. You managed to finagle an entire nation's and even the world's wealth right out from under them. Creating money from thin air and then collecting interest on it while constantly without fail convincing everyone it was to their benefit. All the while they enslaved themselves without one link of one chain. And the large open eye staring at the proles every day, the dedication to me and my house, the very shadow of death, almost makes my heart swell. You can thank me later Mr. O'Brien for all that stolen wealth I let you enjoy all these years. Incidentally, you'll have *plenty* of time to thank me; take my word for it."

Mr. Khul wasn't done yet.

"And let's not leave out the moral relativists. Destroy all truth until the PARTY, that *would* have been you Mr. O'Brien, becomes the truth. Open mindedness, tolerance, *all* truth is relative sounds so good, so philosophical. Aaaah. But if you think about all of it especially that last one for one second it makes no sense. And I know you *know* this is true... *that* last statement *cannot* be true can it? Of course you almost did pull this thing off. Completely take a monopoly on truth and redefine it as you and the Party see fit in an effort to control everything. That's not power, that's insanity Mr. O'Brien. But *that's* what I would love - if I was able to love. After a while, the Party will eat itself alive trying to bring "order". Your "order" will be what you humans call "chaos", *my* kind of order, *my* Great Plan Mr. Obrien. All that will exist will be death, destruction and utter hopelessness; riots, starvation, cannibalism and all sorts of goodies. And no my poor misguided friend there will be no phoenix rising from the ashes of what you believe is your chaos to usher in the Golden Age for you and 500 million of your fellow travelers."

After a brief pause Mr. Khul added, "By the way, this is where that whole Second Coming thing comes in."

Now Mr. Khul's voice took on a slightly jovial tone. "And then all the Party along with the millions of poor souls you helped me deceive will be totally **mine**. Now maybe you can see why those human peasants need a source of absolute truth above the world like God and His Book, for instance - or else "bye bye". But you always knew this didn't you Mr. Obrien? Yet you chose to ignore it, chose the world, chose money and power…chose me….Jesus is *really* going to want to talk to you. Better you than me."

Suddenly O'Brien jumped in and burst out, "Well what about all those famous writers, Orwell, and Aldus Huxley and Thoreau and Emerson? They were all smart, humanists and they didn't believe in God."

Mr. Khul replied smugly to O'Brien's sorry attempt at an argument. "Come on, Mr. Obrien, now you're grasping at straws. You can do better. As I told you someone like yours truly *has* to be the direct opposite of perfect Goodness. And I got to them just like I got to you, Mr. O'Brien. Like you they needed to suppress their very instincts in order to deify themselves. And like you deep down they all knew God exists. But I was able to pull the veil down and blind them all."

O'Brien wouldn't give up. He went on, "Then what about all those intelligent scientists, Darwin, Sagan, Dawkins?"

Mr. Khul gave another measured response as if he had heard all it before. "Really, Mr. O'Brien, the *theory* of evolution? Think about that one. You know damn well that there's *no* way that the *entire* universe and all this organization could have come from an egg, don't you, Mr. Obrien? I mean they used the very intelligence God gave them to justify Him away by saying that all life *and* intelligence sprung from dead *and* mindless slime. The very assumption that God doesn't exist is not from science but from the depths of their own puny corrupted minds. It's all insane; none of it makes sense. Now that's *my* kind of thinking, Mr. O'Brien. And there was no shortage of great scientists I could never deceive because they believed in Him. You know the names, Newton, Kelvin and Pasteur come to mind. But I can't almost thank you enough; you helped me fool many a poor soul with that one. You even helped me grab some of my most hated enemies, those Christians, who foolishly left their faith to throw away huge chunks of the Bible to become more what's the term, open minded if I'm not mistaken."

Mr. Khul knew he had O'Brien checkmated. In fact he knew this for years and now he was taking delight in letting O'Brien know all this as he kept torturing his mind.

So Mr. Khul went on. "Incidentally Mr. O'Brien, how is it you let the theory of evolution get so far? Absolute order out of complete chaos yet at the same time you and the Party continually call me the Great Architect of the Universe? Your entire belief system is little more than a sick joke. You have me pegged as Pan the god of drunkards and chaos AND the Great Geometer of the Universe? Just how stupid are you people?"

Mr. Khul's tone moved from monotone to condescending. "Mr. O'Brien, do you see where I'm going with all this? Well please allow me to continue. This theory of evolution is oh so dear to me."

Mr. Khul continued. "As much as I would love you, if I were capable of love, there are people I would love more than you, Mr. O'Brien. While you caused untold physical misery and death throughout history all of which I almost loved, I really would like to love some of the great deceivers. They get me souls for *my* eternal kingdom. What did you think Jesus was joking when he said not to fear those that could take physical lives but those that could send you to hell? Jesus cannot lie Mr. O'Brien. And He takes things like that *very* seriously. Take this Dawkins guy you mentioned. "The God Delusion"…this guy's almost great. He spends his whole life defending the *theory* of evolution and he's supposed to be a *scientist*? This guy deep down knows that it contradicts every conceivable law of math and science, God's math and science. Order from complete disorder and life from slime? It's completely nonsensical, what a fool. And it gave us just the intellectual license we needed to kill millions and millions. Wanton slaughter, misery, torture, death and destruction, Jacobins, Communists, Nazis, Maoists, hundreds of millions dead... the almost excitement; be still my empty voided heart."

Mr. Khul feigned regret and sarcastically requested, "Oh dear; please do forgive me Mr. O'Brien."

O'Brien gazed but said nothing.

Mr. Khul waited a second or two then simply stated, "Well Mr. O'Brien I see you have nothing to contribute so I'll continue to have the floor."

Mr. Khul, keeping the complete monopoly on the conversation, continued, "Why God would throw such an intellectual like Dawkins into my lap is beyond me. But I'll take him. It's just like that former daughter of mine, that woman of Canaan who Jesus told to take His bread and feed her children instead of throwing it to those dogs. But she said that the dogs still hang around to eat the crumbs that fall from the Master's table. My cohorts and I, we're the dogs, Mr. O'Brien. And we'll take *any crumbs* the Master throws our way. If this Dawkins character can deceive millions to believe that the entire universe came from an egg or some slime and not God, then so be it. And if I can use him to lambaste those putrid Christians out of the realm, the better it is for me. I mean this evolution runs the gamut...an explosion now it's what...the world always existed or something...back to a random explosion...now some are realizing how dumb the whole thing really is and calling it "Intelligent Design" or "Panspermia" and "Ancient Aliens" but they *still* refuse to acknowledge God? Even the guy he defends, Darwin himself, had serious reservations about his *own theory*. This guy's almost my favorite. Call yourself a scientist, sound really smart but in reality make no sense and voila, millions will worship you in the name of science; Godless science that is. And you helped me spread this guy's theories, Mr. Obrien. By getting rid of God, you and the Party became God, or so you thought Mr. O'Brien."

"Our Bohemian friend certainly thought he was God, didn't he Mr. O'Brien?" Mr. Khul inquired.

Mr. Khul didn't wait for a response to his rhetorical question and kept speaking. "And then there's this other kindly gentleman, Mark Booth, who wrote the "Secret History of the World". Ewww, so scary. He sounds so convincing and intellectual. All the ancient mystery religions, the secret societies are mentioned. He even throws Christianity into the mix. With guys like him is where I do my best work, Mr. O'Brien. Throw in some truth, then get those putrid Christians in the mix and voila God is reduced to the level of some pagan god from history. It's just another superstitious religion. Even *he* leans on that ridiculous theory of evolution to make many of his points. He *theorizes* something about ancient fish gods of the old mystery religions and how they really saw evolution way back when or something or other. I don't care. If it reduces Jesus Christ to just another guy or some guy in charge of a pagan religion it almost makes my voided heart swell."

"And it just so happens that these two came about from that Oxford, what a place. You know about Oxford, don't you Mr. Obrien? How could I forget our very own Invisible College, the Great Mystery School and the very foundation of our Ministry of Education and of course where many of your Party cohorts got their start? After our old friend Plato's ideas got to that Cecil Rhodes and those Rothschilds we were really able to set the world on -a Lake of - Fire with perpetual revolutions "for the people" that never benefit anyone except the morticians and gravediggers weren't we, Mr. O'Brien?"

As the talk of the deaths of millions along with wanton destruction continued Mr. Khul became somewhat jocular.

"What, you don't think this is funny? Lake of Fire, hell, don't you get it, Mr. O'Brien? Mr. O'Brien you were laughing just a little while ago aboard the train to Jekyll Island. Geez and they tell me I need to lighten up. Speaking of Oxford that's where one of my favorite Presidents came from. I believe he was one of yours too, Mr. Obrien. Yes that Bill Clinton was great. He did more to help us put the final nail in the coffin of the good 'ol US of Atlantis and usher in our New World Order than any of his cohorts except maybe that Progressive Wilson character. Come to think of it FDR was no slouch either. But this guy will say anything to get elected and then do *our* wishes. And what he did on the once hallowed ground of the House of the formerly Christian nation with that bimbo almost made *me* blush. If George Washington and John Adams weren't in eternal glory with God Himself their rotted bones would be spinning in their maggot infested graves."

Mr. Khul's voice kept its gleeful tone as he continued with his speech. "And that wife of his, she's a real @ on wheels and yet another fine product of our Ministry of Education. I really almost love this woman. She would drink human blood to achieve power. She has that blind lust for power that serves me so well. I mean she could take a seat next to Margret Sanger herself and feel right at home. Of course the more she shoots her mouth off in her do anything path to power she may go too far. Do you agree, Mr. Obrien? As evil as she is she is starting to overplay her hand. I mean one week she's hugging some old woman saying she's a Christian then two weeks later she's trying to outdo that Obama guy on abortion. She wants some kind of village where everyone's equal, to help everyone out. But most smart people know damn well that she won't be happy unless she's mayor of the village. It's not unlike our Communism, Mr. Obrien. Everyone is equal, you were just more equal. Then she's a strong woman…then she's literally crying alligator tears for votes…She's our media darling… She may the next President. But she is really starting to look silly. People may start to wake up and figure this whole scam out, won't they Mr. Obrien? After you're gone I'll have to talk to the Party and maybe think about dumping her. Speaking of that Obama guy, this guy may even serve me *better*. I mean he actually voted *against the Born Alive Infant Abortion Protection Act*…four times. That insatiable bloodlust….be still my empty voided heart. Now with your help I've got these fools a half a step from the Nazis that so many of the brave ones died fighting and they don't even know it!!! This is almost great. Not even that Hillary would go for that one. And that so-called church he believes in. I almost love that place as much as that Catholic Church. It takes a few Christian principles, throws in some pagan worshipping, hangs out with despotic thugs, preaches a thinly veiled Communism and calls itself a Church? And *this* is the guy that will bring the nation together? I'll have to get back to the Party to decide who will serve *my* purposes better. Both seem *oh so* qualified to help bring in *my* Great Plan. What do you think, Mr. Obrien?"

But O'Brien just sat there dumbfounded.

Mr. Khul regained his more sarcastic tone and inquired, "What you don't care anymore?"

O'Brien just stared and listened as Mr. Khul continued his latest diatribe.

"Speaking of that Catholic Church, some of the members are getting rambunctious. It seems they're starting to wonder why they need all that pomp and circumstance and procedures and huge monoliths and the Pope when Jesus Himself said He was the **only** way to Heaven. That Catholic Church has really served me well, Mr. Obrien. It mixes in some real Christian beliefs with a bunch of pagan worship garbage, burns thousands at the stake that don't fall into their line of thinking, enriches itself and then claims the title of Christian. Now the whole world uses the word Catholic interchangeably with Christian. And now many hate the Catholic Church for all its hypocrisy. This is almost great! Queen of Heaven? Saint Anthony? Confession? The Rosary? The Crusades and the Inquisition? Are these guys serious? Jesus Himself plainly warned against idolatry and vein repetition. And I could be wrong but I'm almost certain He would not condone ripping people in half and breaking every bone in their body for simple theological disagreements. And burning people at the stake for having the nerve to read their own Bibles?? I almost love these guys. Deceit has always been the name of the game, has it not Mr. Obrien? I'll have to go have a word with the Pope and tell him to get these people in line. Many of his predecessors listened to me, I'm quite sure he'll be no different. Maybe I can even convince him to be more open-minded. Help save the environment just like those fools at the UN, give to the poor while they live in complete luxury and who knows maybe even somenonsense about how all religions need to work together…they all lead to God…. or god. I almost love it. Jesus Christ is re-labeled and reduced to the same level of a bunch of saints and popes *they* decide on, birthed by the Whore of Babylon and all by people everyone *thinks* are Christians."

"Way to go guys!" Mr. Khul blurted out in his most gleeful tone yet as he raised both his fists to around chest height and clasped them together to accentuate his excitement.

"And that Vatican is one of my favorites. Mr. O'Brien please refresh my memory. Your construction friends, what did you call yourselves, Freemasons, I believe it was, or was it the Templars? It doesn't matter actually. So tell me again why all of you built those hundreds of ornate dare I say almost exquisite edifices and monuments of stone dedicated to yours truly? Please do not tell me you missed the part about God, which would not be me, stating quite clearly He does not reside in temples made with hands or how He abhors worship of hewn stones. I notice He did say the doorways to those beautiful stone houses are but the entrances to Hell. But you just had to step through those gateways, didn't you Mr. O'Brien?"

Mr. Khul added, "In case you have not figured it out yet your covenant with Hell, or yours truly, will be annulled as promised."

Mr. Khul's sarcasm almost forced him to smile as he thanked O'Brien and the Party. "Oh lest I forget thank you kindly for remembering my birthday, March 22 on my favorite monument of all; the one with MY commandments etched in that exquisite granite. I am so humbled; you didn't need to do that."

"Hell, pun most certainly intended, Mr. O'Brien although I almost appreciate the thought, I did not need such grandeur to deceive my elect. Take all these so-called evangelicals with their fancy cars and tens of thousands of herded Christians in their mega churches. They would make my very heart flutter, if I had one. I have the same deal with them that we have, Mr. O'Brien; so you see, you're not alone. Many of their followers will be oh so close to God's Kingdom only to find out they were had by a bunch of charlatans. Almost Christians going to Hell...It's almost as bad as me, except I was *in* the Kingdom. Makes a shiver go down my spineless back...What's the matter, Mr. Obrien? You're not worried about *my* concerns?" Mr. Khul asked.

"What a couple of con artists and tricksters, you and I. But did you actually believe I was really going to let *you* rule over my kingdom, Mr. O'Brien? Be in charge of *my* Great Plan? Be serious Mr. O'Brien; just because I promised them to you does not mean I would actually deliver," Mr. Khul said.

Mr. Khul continued to educate the completely deflated O'Brien. "If you haven't figure it out by now I hate everyone, Mr. Obrien, even you and your ilk who helped me cause so much human misery throughout history. But those Christians I hold a special hatred for. God and the Bible and Heaven; I want every human soul for my dark kingdom. **Mine.** And this Son of God, He cared enough for these cretins to enter my dark world and save as many as would listen. If Jesus Christ were here I'd *almost* piss on Him myself I hate Him so much. By the way you fools did do that and all thanks goes to you, Mr. O'Brien. And we got those foolish Atlanteans to pay for it by what dipping a Crucifix of Him in urine and calling it "Piss Christ" or something. And then claiming it was art. What did you call that one, the National Endowment for the Arts? Dear, dear are *you* guys in trouble. It was bad enough we tossed the Almighty out on his ear…after He helped you all get started in the first place. I mean we started that ACLU running around saying that the detestable founding fathers believed in the separation of church and state while the very courts they brought those putrid Christians in front of took an oath… on *the Bible*? We managed to get His 10 Commandments banned by the Supreme Court…. Who had the same 10 Commandments hanging from their very wall? All the while that putrid country under God was so obviously a gift from Him. I thought the Lord was going to end it right there. But then *you* guys *really* pushed the envelope…Piss Christ?! Not even *I* would dare try that one. Wow. But that *really* got on God's nerves and *nothing* makes me almost happier, Mr. Obrien."

"Thanks for that one, buddy," commented Mr. Khul with mockery.

Mr. Khul studied the steadily deteriorating O'Brien and asked, "It looks like you want to ask me another question. What is it?"

O'Brien finally broke his silence and asked a question that many had. "What about all those millions of poor people whom died under…under…"

Mr. Khul decided to help O'Brien who was really starting to break down. "Under what, Mr. Obrien? Those Communist and Nazi and all those other evil regimes throughout history we created together? I'm not sure, Mr. Obrien."

O'Brien, who thought he was getting the upper hand, asked, "Well how is He going to judge the whole world and every person that ever lived?"

Mr. Khul simply looked at him and in a steady voice tersely replied, "I'm not sure, Mr. Obrien."

O'Brien asked, "What about all the people who never heard of Jesus Christ or worshipped God?"

But Mr. Khul wasn't fazed and simply responded, "Not for me to say, Mr. Obrien. But I'll take whatever crumbs the Lord throws my way."

O'Brien thought he really regained the upper hand and remarked, "Huh, you're not so smart, Satan."

But as usual Mr. Khul was ten steps ahead of O'Brien and his response was immediate. "Well Mr. Obrien it goes something like this. When I foolishly tried to throw God off His throne it took less time than that fake explosion of that fake egg to create the universe for Him to toss my cohorts and me right out of Heaven. God is infinitely good and merciful Mr. Obrien, but believe me – I am speaking the truth with you - on this one: **Do not cross Him**. When I was tossed from Heaven, I was taken out of the loop. Just like those fools who actually listened to me in the beginning, Adam and Eve. So many of your questions I'm not so sure about. But think about it, Mr. Obrien, you're a smart man… sometimes. If God was able to create the *entire* universe including time itself don't you think He has it figured out? Can you comprehend the invention of time itself, Mr. O'Brien? It's impossible even for all those supposedly intellectual scientists who I was able to convince that the only truth that mattered was scientific truth. Professing themselves to be wise they did indeed become fools, Mr. Obrien. *They* jumped through hoops and skirted every real scientific law to "prove" their *theory*. And He is infinitely good so His judgment will have to be perfect. And my former employee that Pharisee Saul did say quite clearly that God would "wink" at a lot of these poor humans' misguided ways. But he did mention something interesting, a warning to stop worshipping their "unknown god." Why that sounds strangely familiar does it not?"

"Worshipping an unknown god…where have I heard *that* one before?" Mr. Khul asked tauntingly.

Mr. Khul continued with a more matter of fact tone. "And of course the Lord does work in mysterious ways. He makes the effort to contact everyone. For some it may be as simple as picking up the right book or meeting the right person. For others they may be exposed to a death of loved one or a scene so grisly that they will have to realize that there *has* to be an exact opposite to all that death and destruction. Or else that death and destruction isn't what the humans call "bad", just like our moral relativism, Mr. O'Brien. Take that Abe Lincoln. He was an Atlantean when that truly meant something as he persevered throughout life. Then he held himself and the US of Atlantis we both hate so much together through that war I almost loved so much; and that you helped me start, Mr. O'Brien. He never realized that the Lord was reaching out for him his whole life. Like that Washington character, the Lord took a real liking to this guy. And then he sees that scene of rotting stinking corpses, which is just like roses to me, at that place in Pennsylvania, Gettysburg I believe it was. And then it clicks. God and infinite goodness has to be real because something must exist that's the exact opposite of what he witnessed after that terrible, at least in his eyes, fight. He becomes a putrid Christian. Speaking of honest Abe, he almost outwitted you and your Party friends, didn't he? He had your cunning, finagling, money-manipulating ways all figured out. Like that detestable Andrew Jackson jerk did. But if he exposed *you* than *my* Great Plan would have been in peril."

"Thanks for getting rid of him," Mr. Khul added.

"Washington. Adams. Lincoln. The Lord really loved this country at one time to grant them such leaders. Now with your Party's help of endless media induced intellectual malaise we've got these mindless zombies electing a fake leader from a bunch of self righteous, megalomaniacal Godless buffoons."

As O'Brien slinked in the chair Mr. Khul spoke on.

"That's all you need to know. It's really not that difficult is it, Mr. O'Brien? It has something to do with what those rotten Christians call faith. Except God made it so simple that faith in Him *is* to be logical -General Revelation I believe He calls it -for those who weren't foolish enough to be deceived by this world and us, that is. I even tried to take Adam and Eve along with all their offspring with me to *my* dark kingdom. The way I saw it, if I could bring down His creation, maybe, just maybe, I could avoid the eternal torment that I know awaits. But just like every putrid human that ever lived God knew my moves before I even *thought* them, Mr. O'Brien. And I did eventually read the Bible. And it's all true. We did the best we could to get rid of it, Communism, Nazism, evolution, secular humanism,

"New" Age, whatever. You for your blind lust for power, me simply because I hate God."

"But God quite wouldn't let us get away with that one would He, Mr. O'Brien?"

Mr. Khul asked, "You were going to say something?"

O'Brien who had been quiet for some time responded, "Umm…so now you're only intention in what's left of your life is to take as many as people to hell with you simply because it irritates God to see anyone have to go? That can't be it. There must be more."

O'Brien paused for a moment then continued, "You can't be that..that…"

Mr. Khul helped him finish as he asked, "What Mr. Obrien?"

O'Brien struggled to get a simple word out. And finally it came as he simply stated, "Evil….uh yeah, that's the word."

Mr. Khul looked at O'Brien squarely and asked, "Can't I? I am in the spirit world what you were trying to achieve in the human world, power and control for the sake of …power and control. You for temporary physical control of deceived humans, me for infinite spiritual control of deceived human souls that foolishly gave up eternity with Him for yours truly. You never cared about all those millions of poor bastards we killed together and *now* you're having second thoughts? Look at you, you're pathetic. You're as pathetic as me, Mr. O'Brien. Our whole existence is based on nothing more than deceit. And in the end that can't win, can it? It will work for a time and on some. Even near the end the Lord knows many will be deceived. But some won't. But we'll have so screwed up and deceived the world, you and me together, that Jesus Christ will once again have to leave

His throne to fix it. And, believe you me He's not coming back as the sacrificial lamb like before."

Mr. Khul then turned and once again looked out the window onto Grimes Square and stared down at the bustling masses far below.

He continued, "Well I've got to get going soon. Unfortunately, I cannot be everywhere at once like the Lord. I've got to go act like an Ascended Master over at the UN… or the spirit of light, an Ancient Alien, cosmic messenger, the Christ, DK the Tibetan, the Count of Saint Germain, Mother Earth or whatever those "New" Age and postmodernist ding-dongs want my cohorts and me to be. *Really? Mother Earth?* Those fools will worship trees, the sky, rocks, sun, moon and stars whatever they want, except God. And I will always make room for them; in fact I make room for *everyone, all applicants accepted.* If they only thought for two seconds their whole deal makes no sense. If everything is God, god becomes everything, everything becomes meaningless and dilute and then nothing. And then God becomes god…just like those Eastern Religion fools. This is all so cute of me, no Mr. Obrien? And best of all I've even been able to snare some of those nasty Christians and those Catholics with these Mother Earth loving lunatics. To think God would allow His creation to be destroyed by another one of His creations. *They* of all people should know much better."

Mr. Khul turned around and looked once again directly at O'Brien. "And you got them *all* started you and your Party friends for that very purpose didn't you, Mr. O'Brien? You thought you controlled them didn't you? You and your Party friends laughing it up behind closed doors at *those* Mother Earth and New Age buffoons who were unwittingly helping you, the mega-capitalists. But all along you were worshipping me too, Mr. O'Brien. What did you think Jesus was kidding when He said you couldn't worship God and mammon, Mr. O'Brien? To me what the hell do I care? Hell, get it Mr. Obrien? Oh come on laugh. That was funny. Where's that spirit of Jekyll Island? Or the day we blasted JFK's head off in broad daylight and blamed it on everyone else but us?"

But O'Brien sat silent. He now realized his fate had been sealed long ago and that his entire life of power and prestige was a ruse.

Mr. Khul went on. "Never mind but I do hope you "Angel of Light-en" up for my party. Mr. O'Brien, don't you get it, "light"? I'm really starting to get a complex here. You guys and those "New" Age fools really thought I was Lucifer, the Angel of Light and I'm really just a dark, deviant scumbag. Come on smile for your Father. Well you'll have *plenty* of time to laugh it up with the rest of your Party at *my* party, trust me."

"The name of my game, Mr. Obrien, is deception, just like yours. But I'm a just a little bit better at it. It's all so ironic isn't it? You manipulate the human world, I manipulate you and the Almighty has been in control all along. You owned the whole world at one time or at least thought you did. At the end of the day the only thing you *really* own is your will. You who owned so much now equal to all those untold millions, those proles, who you *thought* you, controlled. And whose *physical* lives you ruined. Now you'll be equal to all of them, Mr. O'Brien. The Lord did say He is no respecter of persons; just like our invention Communism, how richly ironic. Richly, that's another joke Mr. O'Brien. Mr. O'Brien I'm throwing out my best material but you're not laughing.

This is funny, the Bible isn't for those evangelical idiots, there's deeper meaning there. Where's that smile you had just a little while ago? I'm really starting to get a complex here."

Now sarcasm, condescension and joy combined as Mr. Khul went on.

"Not just a *little* chuckle for "Father"? Or how about a little Illuminating smile?"

Mr. Khul went on but with a slightly more serious tone.

"Anyway, the Lord will judge everyone the same. Now *that's* fair, *that's* Communism, isn't it Mr. O'Brien? There's one minor exception, instead of you being in control the infinitely perfect and fair Lord will rule, and in your case... oh boy. Don't get me wrong. Any philosophy that completely expunges God is a top in my book...which isn't exactly the Lord's Book of Life, believe me. And isn't it further ironic that Karl Marx, the father of Communism who supposedly hated *all* religion worshipped me? If more people had bothered to look into this even a little they might have smelled a rat all along. But you helped me keep them asleep, Mr. O'Brien. It turns out atheistic communism wasn't so Godless after all. No, no correct that, it was *Godless*, just not godless. And my almost favorite, that God bashing *Theory* of Evolution just so happened to come along around the same time. But we were able to deceive all those imbeciles together, weren't we, Mr. O'Brien? You for your blind lust for earthly power and me just because I hate everyone infinitely and nothing makes me almost happier than to see death and misery and most of all millions of souls heading for *my* dark kingdom with no hope of escape."

Mr. Khul wanted to be sure O'Brien got the message and concluded, "Ever."

For a few moments the two looked at each other.

Mr. Khul then revealed, "I'll *really* need to be going soon. I've got some of my evil cohorts, demons I believe those nauseating Christians call them, doing my bidding for me. *That's* the Hierarchy you fools have been so enamored with all this time. But if you want something done right, you have to do it yourself, don't you, Mr. Obrien? You've been awfully quiet. You looked worried. Is everything okay? Well don't worry we'll soon have all the time in the world, and I do mean *all,* to figure it all out."

O'Brien mumbled incoherently.

Mr. Khul returned to a more serious demeanor and asked, "What are you mumbling? Speak your mind man."

O'Brien nervously asked questions he already knew the answer to. "So..so..the Great Plan we all thought we were in control of...it's all ...a...deception? So all those "ancient mystery" religions, the Great Pyramids, Masonry, the Illuminati...you were there all along?"

Mr. Khul tersely replied, "Yes, Mr. Obrien."

O'Brien continued, "So all the history we thought we controlled...the planning...all that private scheming... Oxford...Communism...the CFR... Bilderberg meetings... the Great Plan."

Mr. Khul answered this amazing revelation in workmanlike fashion. "Yes Mr. Obrien it's all for naught."

Mr. Khul went on. "And of course if I was there... can you guess Who was there listening, watching with me? Yikes. He warned in His Book that we tried so hard throughout history to exterminate that the deceived *and* the deceiver are His. And He does not fib, Mr. O'Brien."

O'Brien started to ask a question but faded as he once again knew the answer. "So all of history is...is nothing more than Him watching all along waiting to take the ones who chose to listen to eternal glory and the rest..."

Mr. Khul obliged and responded, "Yes, Mr. O'Brien now you have finally figured it out. From our first attempt at the Great Society back there before the Flood, the next at the Tower of Babel and now the upcoming New World Order you, the Party and I worked so hard to create. Three strikes and you're out, Mr. O'Brien. The Lord has really had it with our shenanigans. By the way, that last one is going to be complete bedlam and not the nice utopia for all mankind under your command you and *your* cohorts tried to pull off so you could enjoy yourselves. Take the worst scenario you can imagine and then multiply it by ten, a thousand, I don't know. I just know that my demons and I, my Hierarchy, will be granted free reign. Just like Mr. Jagger said I am in need of restraint, Mr. O'Brien. Now *that* just might be fun, that's *my* Great Plan you fool. Suddenly those Satanists who loved me outright, why I'll never know nor do I care, every "New" Age moron, those Wiccan freaks, all those fools who were contacting their "spirit guides", "ancient aliens" and "angels of light" or whatever they wanted to call us will be horrified to find out to whom they were really talking all this time. It will be insanity with death and destruction and pain and misery. People will literally go insane as my demons and I run around the earth eating souls and driving people to the brink of Lord knows what without Him restraining us. They will have nowhere to run. The Lord Himself throwing in some of His "goodies" for foolish humans who *still* don't get the hint....Aaaah. Be still, my beating voided heart.

You ever heard the term, be careful what you wish for, Mr. Obrien? Well let's just say a lot of those humans you helped me deceive into secular humanism so called wishing for God to go away so they could run things the "right" way will be granted their wish. It's not unlike those Israeli fools who prayed for an earthly king way back yonder. Don't tell me you glossed over that whole scene as well."

O'Brien could not muster the energy to say anything more. He sat silent as Mr. Khul spoke on.

"We're but chaff on the floor of the barn Mr. O'Brien. To Him Who can simply say the word and both you and I *and* the universe itself will shake to the core, the whole thing is nothing. In the Old Testament, God promised He *will* laugh at our calamity. Now *that's* power. This whole thing doesn't sound good to me. What do you think, Mr. O'Brien? Cat got your tongue? This is your "Father", Mr. Khul, the Illuminated One, why so shy all of a sudden?"

After a short silence Mr. Khul continued.

"No matter, I wish God would end it already; some of these fools we installed as leaders are getting so bad many are actually waking up and listening to what those disgusting Christians have been saying for years. And Lord knows I've spent too much time with you already. Right now time is really getting short, I can hear them playing my tune over at my personal favorite, Metropolis' own St. John's the Divine. That's my cue. Those Party fools you hung around with your whole human existence think they're about to re-create Atlantis. Now the Lord has a much more charismatic body ready and waiting for me so I won't have to keep ghost writing my stuff or pretending to be someone I am not. I haven't been this close to happiness since He let me into that fool Judas Iscariot. Now I can deceive the *whole* world *instantly*. Pity the fools, the Lord is just about out of patience with these human buffoons especially the ones in "New Atlantis". This is my time to really "Shine" like the golden sun light of heaven all you fools thought you were going to acquire after all that "great" work climbing the "stairway to heaven", so called, just like another musical tune the imbeciles listened to daily. Of course you and your Party at that Byzantine Cathedral you built just for me are the worst offenders."

"Suckers all Mr. O'Brien, suckers all."

Mr. Khul went on with a sense of satisfaction in his voice. "Driving those human fools who rejected Him totally insane is the last shot at happiness my Legions and I will have for quite some time. And I don't intend to be late to my last party on Earth brought to all courtesy your Party, Mr. O'Brien."

"You showed me no sympathy, no courtesy, no taste when you merely thought *you* were going to rule my dark world. And now like Mr. Jagger so eloquently stated, I am laying *your* soul to waste, Mr. O'Brien. The Lord is throwing the last batch of deceived souls my way and you know how I feel about that. But since you chose me, Mr. Obrien, I'll give you a choice. Is it going to be a pill like our favorite Bohemian? Or I can have the Ministry of Love prepare the guillotine like they did for that almost lovely Robespierre. It really doesn't matter to be quite honest. When you wake up Mr. O'Brien you'll be looking at the Judge, Jesus Christ Himself. And since you did so much for me, He will be none too happy. I would almost love to be there, nothing makes me almost happier than to see *Him* angry. But at the same time I don't want to be in the same *universe* when *He's* mad. So good luck with that one, Mr. O'Brien, I'm sure I'll be busy that day."

Mr. Khul concluded in an upbeat manner.

"But then you and your Party are *all* cordially invited to *my* party. Along with the millions and millions of poor souls you helped me deceive. And there we'll have *plenty* of time together, trust me. Much more than the 13.7 billion, 15 billion, 100 billion whatever years those idiotic evolutionists, my almost favorite souls, think they needed to prove their non-provable theory; much, much more. And when you think my party finally ends and you run for the door to escape and open it…it starts up all over again…and again. It's just like another "Rock n Roll" song, we are programmed to receive, you can check out any time you like but you can *never* leave…Now go take your pill Mr. O'Brien. The other Party boys and girls will be joining you shortly at *my* party. And our old Party friends, Plato, Cecil, JP, Chuck, Karl, Joe Stalin, Peg Sanger and her Bohemian friend, Alice Bailey, the "New" Age Madame, the Warburg brothers, the Rockefeller clan and their friends the Huxleys, Sagan, Andy Carnegie and last but certainly not least those almost delectable Rothschild boys will *all* be waiting for you."

O'Brien had nowhere to go. He couldn't leave or the Party would have him arrested and executed. He was done and he knew it. He quietly swallowed the little blue pill.

As he was leaving Mr. Khul concluded with a devilishly cordial wish for O'Brien.

"Now I'm really late…talk to you soon, have a nice trip…"

Printed in the United States
By Bookmasters